BIG**FAT**

Client

Hedonist

Hedonist

CONTENTS

BIG FAT CLIENT

* *Jamie* *

"Hello, is this Jamie? Eve, this side. I'm calling to confirm our appointment for this afternoon."

My heart is already racing; has been ever since I booked the session yesterday. As a result, I can't get a damn word out. I just stare at the phone in utter terror, as if that will fix it.

"Hello? Are you there? Can you hear me?" Eve asks.

I close my eyes and take a deep breath. "Yep. Yeah. Confirmed."

"Great, so I'll see you at four!" The line goes blank before I can say anything else. Just as well, because nothing sensible was forthcoming.

Ugh. I hate this. If I'm going to be this terrified by a simple phone call, then what on earth will happen when she gets here?

Once she sees what she's up against, she'll regret ever taking the job. And I'll see it written on her face, and feel utterly guilty for subjecting her to my presence.

A cuddle therapy session. What a fucking stupid idea that was.

I first found out about this service in a documentary I saw on TV. It featured a warm, maternal woman in her fifties who explained what it was like to be a professional cuddle therapist and how so-called contact therapy can benefit people suffering from a whole range of conditions.

A whole range of conditions. Sounds like me in a nutshell.

From the depression to the anxiety to the suicidal ideation and the food addiction. I seem to have developed a little bit of everything over the years. And it's not that I haven't tried to figure things out. Talk therapy was a bust. Self help groups as well. I've read the books and watched the videos and done what I could, but to no avail. I just hadn't tried *this* yet. Because I didn't know it existed.

And a part of me feels like I don't deserve it anyway.

Don't expect too much, I tell myself. *She's a human being, not a miracle worker.*

My phone buzzes, startling me so much that I almost drop the thing. There's the confirmation email, which I open with trembling fingers.

I'm sure it's just a form email, but the tone is friendly and conversational, as if the woman, Eve, herself had written it. It has a few sections in it, starting with a short paragraph about what cuddle therapy really is, what to expect from your first session, and a bold and underlined note that although it's all 100% platonic, mutual consent between the practitioner and client is of the utmost importance. ' *If either party is uncomfortable at any time, they have the right to stop.* '

That's fair enough, but it also just convinces me that she's going to run as soon as she sees me. The state I'm in, I'm not exactly easy on the eyes. And to have to *touch* me is probably too much to ask of the average person.

But, it's too late to cancel. Wouldn't be the first time I'm rejected based on my size and appearance, so I ought to be used to it by now.

My phone call with Jamie didn't go how it was supposed to. I was supposed to call him to refer him to someone else or cancel. As a newly qualified cuddle therapist, my supervisor insisted I avoid scheduling home visits with male clients for now. At least until I get some experience under my belt.

But the note Jamie had written on the booking form spoke to me on a deeper level. I feel like I can really help him, which is why I got into this line of work in the first place.

So, when I called him up and heard the short panicked breaths on the other end, I didn't have it in me to refuse. Plus, we have systems in place for this. To keep us safe during home visits.

If anything untoward happens, I'll just hit the panic button on my phone, and someone from Compliance will call the client's phone immediately, giving me the chance to get out of there. Similarly, if I don't check in the moment my session ends, they will contact the client immediately to ensure my safety. Plus, I'm being tracked by GPS as long as I'm clocked in. No big deal. At least that's how it was explained to me during one of the many seminars I've had to sit through to get to where I am.

I'm just going to a 34 year old man's house to spend a 45 minute session with my hands all over him. What could possibly go wrong?

Still, I'm nervous. Because the story on his booking form was so heart wrenching, I really want to do right by him. I want to make a difference. I'm convinced I can, I just hope I can express myself well enough to get through to him.

These are the thoughts going through my mind as I get ready, pack up my bag, and make the trip across town to his place. After I find parking, and make my way inside the apartment complex, I'm getting increasingly tense. It probably isn't a good idea to put this much pressure on myself. At this rate, I'm going to need some cuddle therapy myself, just to calm down.

Deep breaths, girl! He's probably more scared than you are!

Although that's likely, the thought doesn't help. It only makes me more nervous, because it means there's even more pressure on me to do this right.

I ring the doorbell a few minutes early and 'clock on' using the company app.

"Hi, Jamie? It's Eve. I'm here for our appointment," I call out, trying to keep my tone light and cheerful.

Some movement can be heard inside, then finally, the door unlocks and opens just part of the way. I can't quite see inside. It's a little dark, and my eyes haven't adjusted to the dim lighting inside the building yet.

"I'm a little early. Hope you don't mind," I say, while pushing the door open a little further and peeping in.

There he is, waiting just inside, without saying a word. Jamie is a large man, as expected. His problems, as outlined in the intake form, suggested as much. Food addiction, anxiety, agoraphobia. All this tracks perfectly with the morbidly obese man staring at me like a deer caught in headlights. But what I hadn't expected was how his eyes would captivate me and draw me in. So, we're supposed to be cuddling. What's *that* going to feel like?

"May I come in?" I ask, remembering my training. Boundaries and consent are important.

He clears his throat, but doesn't say anything.

"You've read the confirmation email? Remember that I'm here to help. You call the shots, okay?" I say.

He nods and shuffles backwards through the cramped hallway and into the living area. I'm taking that as an invitation, so I step inside and close the door behind me.

His place is… interesting. Not quite hoarder levels of clutter, but not exactly minimalist either. It's obvious that he's been collecting *things* to make up for the lack of people in his life. That's okay, I'm not here to judge. As per Joy--my supervisor with the rather ironic first name-- what I *am* here to do though, is observe all I can about the client to put into my report later.

"Please," he says. "Sit." His voice sounds forced. Tense. He's obviously nervous.

I smile at him and take a seat on the sofa, patting the empty space next to me to get him to join me. He hesitates for a moment, then sits beside me, causing the couch cushion to dip down all the way at his end.

"So, I'm Eve. Nice to meet you." I stick out my hand in his direction, which he shakes reluctantly while mumbling his name. Jamie. Yep. His clammy skin suggests he's terrified.

I keep holding onto his hand after our greeting for as long as he doesn't try to pull away. He doesn't. He just stares at both of our hands, resting on the small section of empty cushion between the two of us.

"I want you to know that if at any point you're uncomfortable and you want me to stop whatever I'm doing, just say so, okay?"

He scoffs. "I was uncomfortable before you even got here."

I smile and make eye contact with him. "It's okay. This is awkward. I get it."

"Yeah. Awkward." He smiles briefly and looks down at our hands again.

"But it also feels kind of nice, doesn't it?" I say, gently squeezing his hand a little, just like I was taught during training. Don't know if it's nice for him, but for me, it's giving me a little kick. Simply holding hands is a vastly underrated activity. Plus, I don't know what it is exactly, but Jamie has captivated my attention completely.

"I'm sorry," he mumbles.

"What for?"

"My sweaty hand."

That makes me grin. "I thought it was mine that was sweaty," I lie.

He looks up at me again with a puzzled expression on his face.

"Maybe you want to begin by telling me what made you book this session? What you want to get out of it," I ask.

He shrugs and stares off at nothing in particular. "I just… Nothing else has worked."

"The way this usually works is, there's obviously a lot of touching. Cuddling. Whatever feels right. But it works best if we talk as well."

"Talk about what?"

"Whatever's on your mind. Like maybe you want to tell me a little bit about your background. Your story."

"Talk therapy hasn't worked for me," he remarks.

"I'm not a therapist. I'm just a person who's here for you. Who cares about what you're going through."

He shakes his head. "You're making it sound like I've lived through some kind of tragedy. I haven't."

"It's not a competition. We're all going through *something*. And I'm here to listen, and to support, and to offer comfort and affection when you're ready."

Jamie sighs deeply and looks at me with a skeptical frown on his face. "It's contradictory."

"What is?"

"Hearing you say you're someone who cares, but then we just met ten seconds ago. And I'm paying you to be here."

He has a point, and yet, it's 100% true. I've always had trouble keeping my empathy under control and that's gotten me into trouble before.

"Consider that both can be true at the same time. We've only just met. And I still care. I started caring the moment I read your intake form."

He exhales sharply through his teeth. "Fuck. I forgot about that," he whispers.

"I guess the point I'm trying to make is. You can talk to me if you want. Or we can just sit here and hold hands. It's entirely up to you. But--" I glance over at him. He's sitting there with his eyebrows scrunched together and his lips pressed together tightly.

"What?"

"Correct me if I'm way off, but you look tense. Like you really need a hug. Maybe it's been a while since the last one of those, huh?"

His face contorts for a split second. He's trying his best to keep his emotions in check. That's yet another thing we could work on together. If he'll let me.

"May I?" I ask, turning towards him in my seat and holding my other arm out in his direction.

He presses his lips into a tight line and glances at me. Moisture is collecting in the corner of his eyes. *Purging,* they called it in training. He's due for some purging of pent up emotions.

Although this was something I was most worried about encountering in a real session, I know it's necessary. In for a penny…

I'm still trying to work out the logistics of me and my five-foot-five frame trying to wrap my arms around this absolute giant of a man, when he mouths: "Okay."

I figure, if I go for the shoulders, that'll be most effective. So, I get into my knees beside him and, letting go of his hand, I place both my hands on his shoulders, drawing him in closer, until he yields.

A deep shiver passes through his back as I tighten my grip around him and he rests his head against mine. It's amazing. Profound. This is exactly the sort of thing I had in mind when I signed up for this job. It's getting me all emotional. Hopefully he won't notice.

"I've got you," I whisper, while caressing his shoulder with one hand, and the back of his neck with the other.

He sighs once. Twice. Then he tenses up again and tries to pull away.

"I can't," he grumbles.

I loosen my grip on him and lean back just enough to look him in the eye. More tears have collected. This is an emotional moment, and it's obvious he doesn't know how to deal.

"It's okay, Jamie." I try to smile.

He stares at me with both eyebrows raised up high. "You're crying. I'm sorry."

His breaths start to quicken while he tries to swallow his emotions, and fails.

I want to tell him I'm only tearing up because I can feel the gravity of what he's dealing with, but I don't. People tend to think that's weird.

"Seeing as I'm already crying, you might as well join me. May I hug you again? Feel free to hug me back." I say.

He pauses, but then gives in. This time, I can feel him surrender more completely. He rests his head against my shoulder and tentatively places his arms around me. I melt into him and grip him confidently around his shoulders.

His back shudders again. And again. Here we go. The purge has begun.

Tears are streaming down my face too now. It's beautiful to be able to do this for someone. A perfect moment.

The only trouble is, all this cuddling is affecting me so deeply, I'm in danger of forgetting my role. I'm supposed to be conducting this session, and yet, here I am, in the arms of a stranger, weeping into his shoulder. Hard as I may try, I end up releasing all the doubts and worries I've had ever since I completed my training a couple of weeks ago.

I remember so keenly how I got here. My previous job; the rejection I felt when I was told I wasn't right for it… I had hoped that *this* would allow my strengths to shine, rather than drag me down again.

While this isn't my first session, it feels so much more intense than the others I've done. Like there's so much hinging on it. If I fuck up, it won't just lead to a bad review, and a bollocking from Joy, it'll actually affect someone's wellbeing. I couldn't live with myself if I thought I'd ruined someone's chances at recovery.

"I'm sorry," he stammers in between sniffles. "I'm so sorry."

"Baby, it's okay. Feel your feelings. Let it all out."

Fuck. Did I literally just call him 'baby'? Luckily he seems to have not noticed, because now he's all-out bawling.

And I'm still holding him. Still comforting him. Still dealing with my own emotions brought on by his release. I rub his back, which keeps on trembling with every breath. I caress his hair, and cuddle my head against his. He seems to like that, because he reciprocates.

It occurs to me that I've never hugged a really fat person before. Not including older female relatives while growing up. Not like this; not as an adult and not a man. And it's… It's really nice. Different. Tactile.

How his body accommodates mine. How I can squeeze my arms around him firmly without feeling even a hint of bone anywhere. I love it. It's like he was made for this.

It makes me wonder what else he was made for, but I swallow that thought pretty quickly.

Arousal is normal, I repeat what the instructor said during training in my head. *But you don't get to entertain it. Ever.*

I just… I can't help but think, if this is how he reacts during a simple hug, what would he be like in bed? My empathy being off the charts as it is, that would be like… emotion porn. The most alive anyone could ever feel. A far cry from the sorts of guys you find cruising for chicks on a Friday night. The sorts of guys I've had the misfortune of encountering before… Closed off and stunted and cold.

No, sex with Jamie in his current state would be like… It would be pure. Blissful. Spiritual, almost.

"I almost cancelled," he whispers, distracting me from my inappropriate fantasies.

Oh good. Talking is good.

"I'm glad you didn't."

"I'm really sorry. I don't know what happened." He tries to sniffle the last of his tears away, but then, he starts crying again.

"This is good. Everything is progressing exactly how it's supposed to," I say, while shuffling from one knee to the other. This position is starting to get tiring.

He seems to notice and instinctively holds me tighter to keep me steady. It's the sweetest thing.

"You're purging whatever emotions have been stuck for a while."

"It's inappropriate."

I smile and shake my head. What's inappropriate is all the filthy thoughts I've been having while he's been ugly-crying in my arms.

"Let me guess, you think boys shouldn't cry?" I ask.

"Nobody likes a cry baby."

"Guess what. I still like you."

He pulls away and stares at me through tear-stained lashes. Only now do I notice the depths of his dark brown eyes. It's like peering into his soul.

"You don't even know me."

His remark makes me question myself again. Fuck. Earlier I called him 'baby' and now I told him I like him. I guess this is why Joy didn't want me to take this session.

But the longer I look at him, the more I realise how I feel. I mean every word.

* *Jamie* *

I don't know how it happened. One moment I drunkenly sent a booking request to a professional cuddling service, and the next, I've got this beautiful girl in my flat. Kneeling on the sofa next to me, her arms wrapped around my neck, and telling me she *likes* me.

She couldn't possibly.

All within the span of fifteen minutes, we went from me barely getting a word out in front of her, to her holding her hands and both of us crying in each other's arms.

When I booked this session, I didn't know what I was expecting, but it certainly wasn't this.

And the longer I look into her moist green eyes, the harder it gets to remind myself that this is a service I'm *paying* for. This isn't a genuine connection of any kind. She doesn't *care* about me. The only reason she's even at my place is because I went on a website to order her here. Like Chinese food, or pizza.

But the way she's looking at me... It tries to convince me of a different truth. She must be a saint, not just to do this work, but to do it so well I literally can't tell that she's acting.

And now that the tears are starting to dry up, my body also can't tell the difference. Because certain parts of my anatomy have started to wake up to her presence in a most inconvenient way.

No wonder I was stunned to silence when she arrived. She's nothing like the woman I saw on TV. Late twenties or thirty at the most. Petite. Gorgeous. Not a mother-figure in any way shape or form. Her wavy brown hair, tied into a bun, would look amazing open and framing her pretty face. Pinkish lips, slightly parted, while she catches her breath, so tempting I want nothing more than to reach out and caress my thumb against them.

And her body. Good lord. Curves in all the right places. Moments ago, those perky breasts were crushing up into me. I had my arms around that perfect waist.

What were they thinking, sending this goddess into my home? We're mismatched like Princess Leia and Jabba the Hut.

Platonic touch, the website said. *Platonic!* How on earth am I supposed to keep my feelings platonic, when she's literally the most attractive woman I've ever seen? It goes against every instinct; every urge. It goes against nature itself.

She reaches for my face, taking my breath away again. With the back of her hand, she wipes the tears off my cheeks and smiles. That smile. It could start wars and end civilisations.

"How about you lie down in my lap and tell me about yourself?" she says. "I'd like to get to know you better. If that's okay, of course."

My heart twists painfully in my chest. That's right.

We don't know each other yet. And there's not a damn thing about me that's worth finding out about either.

But still, if that's what she wants, then who am I to refuse?

You're the client, you moron! She doesn't want it, you're paying for every second of this!

Still, I nod in agreement and watch her as she gets comfortable on her end of the couch. Then she waves at me and guides me down. It's awkward, trying to manoeuvre my large body into position like this. She keeps watching me in silence, while I try to be casual and fail.

At first, I end up on my back, which makes it hard to breathe. Then, I try to turn onto my side, having to shove and heave parts of my own body out of the way just to get positioned right.

By the time I'm done, I'm out of breath and bright red with shame.

"This is just weird. Forget it," I grumble, but before I get the chance to struggle back up again, her hand settles on my head and I can't find the will to move.

"But it's still nice, right?" she asks, while caressing my hair. "Just relax."

It feels so good. Words can't describe it. I close my eyes and breathe, deeply in and out, while trying to will my rock solid cock back down. To no avail. God, as soon as she leaves, I'm going to have to do something about this. Find some relief, no matter how wrong and disgusting it is.

Her other hand ends up on my shoulder, and I

instinctively reach out and hold it. So small and seemingly so fragile. She squeezes mine, and my heart skips a couple of beats.

In fact, my heart has been racing throughout, but what had started off as fear has morphed into sheer lust and excitement. It's a nice, bubbly feeling. One which I wouldn't mind feeling more often.

"So, who are you, Jamie? What do you do; what do you like?" she asks.

I wish I could see her face, but soon her hand finds its way onto my forehead; caressing, massaging various pressure points. It feels so natural, my eyes snap shut and that's how they remain.

I clear my throat, trying to find the words to answer her questions, but all I can think to say is something completely different.

"I wanted to cancel this session. But I couldn't get the words out on the phone." I sigh.

She keeps massaging that pressure point between my eyebrows, as well as the spots on either side of my nose.

"You were worried about how it would go, right? That's perfectly normal. To be honest, I was a bit worried too."

"Were you?" I suppose, looking at me, anyone would be worried.

"I'm not supposed to tell you this, but I'm kinda new at this. Though I did work as a counsellor for a while before this, so there's that..."

"I wouldn't have known," I whisper. "You're perfect."

Really. She's a natural.

"Joy--my supervisor--she told me I wasn't supposed to do home visits with male clients until I get more experience. I was supposed to refer you to someone else." Her thighs tense underneath me. "You can't tell anyone, okay? I'll get into trouble."

"I won't tell. Promise." Her confession is about to make me cry again. "But… why didn't you? Refer me."

"Because…" She sighs and starts caressing my neck, and the base of my skull.

Damn, that feels good. I can feel my shoulders and back relax more and more as I almost melt into her and sink deeper into the sofa underneath me.

"Because I read what you'd written, and it was like you were calling out directly to me. I knew I could do some good here, you know?"

None of that makes any sense. Then again, I don't even remember what I'd written. I was pretty drunk last night. I don't know what comes over me, but her candidness must be inspiring me to tell the truth as well.

"I barely remember what I wrote. It's all a bit of a haze."

She chuckles softly. "Do you want me to tell you?"

I shrug. I'm not sure. It's bound to be humiliating. But I'm feeling kind of high and courageous right now, so I ask for the short & sweet version.

"You wrote that you've been stuck at home and dealing with depression and loneliness and anxiety, and you didn't see any way out, because other therapies haven't worked for you. In fact you ended your comment with the thought that this was all a load of shit and wouldn't do you any good either."

"That sounds pathetic. Not like a person I would want to go and meet," I complain.

She clicks her tongue. "It sounds *human*. And, I guess I thought it would mean that you'd be gentle with me. Considering we're both new at this."

I snuggle into her thigh and smile. "I can be gentle."

She laughs and runs her fingers through my hair. "I can see that."

This whole situation is so unexpectedly nice, I hardly know how to contain my happiness. If I'm not careful, I might just lose myself and imagine that we're just regular people, hanging out together on a Saturday afternoon. When nothing could be further from the truth. Neither of us fit the word: 'normal'. I'm my own pathetic self, and she's… She's extraordinary.

"Do you want to tell me how long you've been having trouble with anxiety?" she asks.

I almost choke on my own breath. No, I really don't. Then again, I'm definitely not running the risk of ever impressing this magnificent woman, so what have I got to lose?

"Oh. Years." Decades.

"Did it start during puberty or before?"

I take a deep breath and try to keep my nerve. "It's been a problem for as long as I can remember. I didn't have what you might call a happy childhood."

It's not a secret, and still it feels like such a shameful thing to admit. So cliché. *Oh, kids used to bully you, did they? Your daddy never loved you, so you tried to eat yourself to death? Grow the fuck up!*

"I'm sorry to hear that," she says, while leaning over me and kissing my hair.

Jesus. What on earth am I supposed to do with this? How I wish she'd kiss me on the lips instead.

"It was a long time ago," I mumble.

"Is it? Or does it still hurt like it was only yesterday?" One of her hands is again caressing my hair in slow, even strokes. The other rests on my upper arm.

"I try not to think about any of that stuff," I say gruffly.

"I understand. What do you tend to think about?"

I exhale deeply and try to get my racing heart under control again. Her questions are starting to freak me out. Like she's picking at scabs that haven't had the chance to heal yet. How stupid. My parents aren't even around anymore; this is all ancient news.

"I don't. I try to take every day as it comes."

"Mhm." Her tone is sweet and light, but I know she disapproves of my answer.

A few moments of silence pass between us. If I try hard enough to keep my own breathing under control, I can just about hear hers.

"How's your sleep?" she asks me.

"Fine, after a few drinks," I lie. I don't remember the last time I had a good night's sleep. What's the point in telling her all this, though? She's not going to wave a magic wand and fix my sleep apnoea as well.

"You know, they fired me from my previous job for

being 'too sensitive'." She makes air quotes around the last two words as she speaks and shrugs. Then, her hands are back on me, where they belong.

I turn my head just enough to be able to see her. Her eyes are already on me when I do.

"From the counselling job?"

She nods, while maintaining eye contact. It's obvious that she feels sore about it, which affects me a little too.

"You're making it sound like that's a bad thing," I say.

"Isn't it?" She caresses the side of my face with the back of her hand. Yet another thing I don't think anyone has ever done to me. It's beautiful.

"Getting fired, yeah, that's bad. Being too sensitive? Who the hell wants to spill their guts to an emotionless robot? This was exactly the problem I've had with my previous therapists."

"See! That's what *I* said. I'm glad we're on the same page. But apparently, everyone else thinks that a counsellor should never appear human. Because then nobody will trust their advice anymore."

Oh, we're definitely on the same page. It's so weird, as well.

Objectively I know that what she's doing is highly unorthodox. The little titbits of information she's shared with me, I can see how that would come across as inappropriate. Too sensitive. Maybe even a little needy.

But I'm hanging on every word of hers anyway. And I'm actually starting to *feel* something out of the ordinary. I'm starting to feel a kind of kinship with her that I haven't felt before. Like maybe I'm not the only one who deals with crippling insecurities and anxieties. Even someone as seemingly perfect as her has a tendency to do the same. It's refreshing.

"You're very easy to talk to, if it helps."

She grins. "Be sure to put that in the feedback form they'll email you."

My heart sinks. Oh yeah. This is still just a transaction. Basic human connection in exchange for money.

"Jamie?" God, I love hearing her say my name. I wish I could hear her say it in entirely different circumstances.

"Yep."

"If you like, you can touch me too."

Her invitation shocks me, just like it did initially when she invited me to hold her.

"I am touching you," I remark, squeezing her hand.

"Right, I mean, if you want to get closer. We can cuddle again, you know?"

I shake my head. Not because I don't want to, but just because I have no idea what she's talking about. "How?"

She gestures at me to turn around a little more, and face her, which I struggle to do. Then, in what looks like a minor contortionist move, she leans over and onto me, resting her head on my arm which I'd laid across my belly. I instinctively put my other arm around her too.

She sighs and smiles contently. "This is nice, right?"

Nice. Yeah. And since her boobs are once again pressed into the side of my body, it's also infuriatingly sexy. Never in my life have I craved a wank as much as right this very moment.

"Talking and counselling is one thing. But what made you want to do *this* with random strangers?" I blurt out. I don't even mean random strangers. I'm sure most are absolutely fine. I mean why would she want to do this with a guy like me.

She grins at me. How does she look so convincingly happy all the time?

"I guess you could call me a 'hugger'. My main love language is touch and affection. Once I heard that you can do this fulltime and pay my bills with it, well, pfft. It was a no-brainer!"

Her *love language?* What does *that* mean? But she does seem pretty damn pleased to be here. Weirdly.

"I'm just not used to it. We weren't big on hugs at home."

"Yeah, a lot of people aren't. But you can't beat that oxytocin high from a really good cuddle session. It's like oxygen for the heart and soul."

A lot of what she says sounds fru fru to me. And yet, I believe every word. This is amazing. It's the most beautiful experience I've ever had. And I owe it all to Eve, going rogue and ignoring her supervisor's instructions.

Somewhere in her stuff, a phone goes off.

Her expression changes just slightly. Was that disappointment I saw?

"That's the alarm. Unfortunately, our session has come to an end."

Now it's my turn to be disappointed. "Oh."

"I really enjoyed spending this time with you," she says. I can't imagine why.

"Yeah, it was... " Amazing. Mind blowing. Life-changing?

"And I think we made some great progress in a really short time. I'd love to see you again for another session. What do you think?"

How much to have her move in with me permanently? God, I wish I was joking. "Uhh."

"Think about it. If you use the link from the feedback email, you can choose whether you want to see me again, or someone else from the agency."

This is such a weird discussion to have, while I'm still cradling her in my arms and she's still lightly caressing my hair.

"Oh, no. I definitely want you again!" That came out... wrong.

She smiles another one of her bright, happy smiles at me. "I'm so glad to hear it. Thank you!"

I loosen my arm around her, and she starts to sit up. Then, it's my turn to struggle and fight, just to get somewhat upright.

Just like that, all the contentment and bliss is forgotten, and I'm deeply ashamed again. My face has heated, my brow is sweaty; even my ears are glowing, it feels like.

Luckily, Eve hasn't noticed, because she's already

pulled her phone out of her bag and is tapping away at the screen.

"Ooo-kay." She glances up at me, smiling again. "That's it. I've clocked out."

Right. Because as profound as it was for me, the time we spent together was just a job to her. Obviously.

But then, why is she still looking at me? Why doesn't she just run already?

"Maybe you can help me out. Where's a good place to buy some groceries around here? I want to make sure I'm fully stocked so I don't have to go out tomorrow," she says.

I frown. I don't know what I was expecting her to say, but that wasn't it. "There's a small supermarket just at the end of the block, uhh…"

"Great! And are there any takeaways nearby? I'm not sure I feel like cooking tonight."

This is my moment to shine. It takes a bit of effort, but I do my best to get up quickly, and head across the room to pick up a stack of menus from one of the many bookshelves lining my modest living room.

"Take your pick," I tell her, while handing her my considerable collection.

"Oh, wow! Thanks!" She grins at me and starts leafing through, while mumbling little comments to herself. "Nope, not Chinese… Just had Italian the other night… Oh, Thai! This any good?"

"Their Pad Thai is the best in the area," I say. I should know. I'm a regular customer.

She takes a picture of the address and hands me the

menus back. "Okay, then I guess I'll make a move, before the parking meter maxes out."

"Okay." I'm just standing there, menus still in hand, when she does a most unexpected thing.

She walks towards me, stands up on her tippy toes and wraps her arms around me. I hold my breath and close my arms while she squeezes me tight, and plants a soft peck on my cheek.

"It was lovely to meet you, Jamie. Hope to see you again soon!" She pulls back and grins at me. "Take care of yourself, alright?"

Although I'm stunned, I still hear myself mumble a few pleasantries. "Okay, thanks. See you."

Only after she leaves, and the door closes behind her, can I breathe easy. Jesus. What the fuck just happened? I reach for my face, where my skin still zings where her lips touched me. Of all the scenarios I had in my head, I never thought my first so-called professional cuddle session would turn out quite like this.

* Eve *

I'm back home, on my couch, balancing a plate of Thai food on my thighs, while simultaneously tapping away at the keys of my laptop. My report is coming together quickly. The sooner I get it done, the sooner I can binge watch some Netflix.

My session with Jamie was a great success, at least according to me. Hopefully his feedback will echo that.

The experience confirmed everything I had

suspected right from the moment I saw his booking. I *can* help him, definitely. But at the same time, I'm having a hard time compartmentalising everything that happened between us.

While I was getting swept up in the moment, I did that thing again that got me into trouble before. I opened up and shared things I should never have shared.

My own doubts. My own emotions.

Sure, I was doing it with a purpose--at least that's what I told myself at the time. And it did have the desired effect: getting Jamie to feel comfortable with me and sharing more about himself too. But at the same time, the experience opened up a whole host of feelings I wasn't ready for.

First of all, there was the unexpected arousal. They'd touched upon this in training, but I never thought it would happen quite like this. With Jamie's large body pressed up against me, and his hands on my back, feverish desire had hit me like a freight train.

He's so unlike all the men I've dated or slept with before, I never would have expected it. And still...

Maybe I need to rethink the kind of men I date. From now on I'm definitely going to seek out men with a bit of meat on their bones! Nothing else will do.

I'm just about done with the report, when my phone rings. As soon as I see the screen, I roll my eyes. Joy.

"Hi!" I try to sound cheerful while answering.

"Eve. What did I tell you?"

"Umm…"

She sighs angrily. "I told you: don't do home visits with men. Especially not first-time clients."

"Right."

"I thought I'd made myself very clear. Imagine my surprise when I see a feedback form come in for you from a young man named Jamie, who had his first session this afternoon."

I pinch the bridge of my nose and close my eyes. "Joy, I can explain."

"You're bloody lucky it's a glowing review, young lady!"

"I had intended to refer him to someone else, but when I called him up to do just that, I changed my mind," I say.

"The rules exist for a reason."

I roll my eyes again. "Joy, I respect your opinion; I really do. But I checked the handbook, and nowhere does it say what you're telling me, leading me to believe that it's more of a guideline than a rule."

She scoffs angrily. "This is the problem with your generation. You all think you know better!"

"In this instance, I felt I could make a real difference. That's why I'm doing this job in the first place."

"You're making a difference with everyone. That's the point. Someone else would have made a difference too."

"I felt that my counselling background--" I say.

"Correct me if I'm wrong, you were fired from that job, weren't you?"

"Not because I wasn't good at counselling. I just

wasn't a good fit--"

"Make sure you follow the rules going forward, or you won't be a good fit here either. Do you understand me?" Joy threatens.

My heart is racing. God, I'm pissed off. Who does she think she is? Nowhere in the handbook did it say I couldn't have taken Jamie on as a client! And as it is, my contract says I'm self employed. Like an Uber driver. Who the fuck is she to decide whether or not I keep on working for the agency?

Despite all this, I grit my teeth and force myself to answer. "I understand."

"So what I want you to do next week--the client has already booked his next session with you--is to convince him to try someone else going forward."

That's the last thing I want. And I'm sure Jamie doesn't want that either. Still, the fact that he rebooked me so quickly makes me smile through my frustration.

"What if he doesn't agree?" I ask.

Joy scoffs. "If you're as good at counselling as you say you are, then you'll change his mind."

With that warning, she hangs up on me. I'm so furious, I keep glaring at the darkened screen of the phone, while waiting for my heart rate to come back down.

What the actual fuck? I conducted a session. We followed all the rules. Jamie made so much progress, within such a short timeframe. And he's so satisfied, he's booked his next session already. And yet, Joy still isn't happy? What does she want, really?

I'm helping someone who really needs it *and* I'm getting great reviews and repeat business for the agency. Isn't that the whole point?

* Jamie *

Time might fly when you're having fun, but it's a stagnant pit of despair when you're waiting for your next session. A week has never felt so long.

After Eve left on Saturday, it took me a good half an hour just to wrap my head around what had happened. And still, I spent the night in a daze of confusion, going over the events of that one session with her until I'd dissected and analyzed every second of it at least a dozen times.

She told me she liked me. She didn't mean it, but every time I replay that part of our conversation in my head, I still feel a little high. The way she talked to me made me feel like her equal. Like I wasn't crazy. Or unlikable. Like I wasn't alone in this world after all.

And then there was how she touched me... Without a hint of hesitation or repulsion. It was the stuff dreams are made of. Or, in my case, daydreams. Which always end the same way: with me rocking an erection so persistent, my feverish attempts at relieving it have been largely unsuccessful.

No sooner so I finish jerking off and catching my breath, do I feel that same dull ache return for an encore.

I don't know how many times I've wanked this

week, only that it was often enough to make me raw and sore. So now I'm not just desperately horny, I'm also throbbing painfully every time the memory of cuddling with Eve makes a reappearance in my mind's eye. Which is often. Every day and every night.

By Thursday, I'm having mixed feelings about this. I'm desperate to see her again, of course. But at the same time I feel more unworthy than ever. Because every single time I've indulged my dirty fantasies about her, I've sullied the beautiful experience she had gifted me.

It was supposed to be a *cuddle session.* Nothing more. She doesn't deserve to have a guy like me lusting over her like this, does she? It's supposed to be *platonic*, dammit!

As such, I'm in a good mood to cancel. Again. But the sheer thought of it fills me with dread. Because if I never see Eve again, I'll never feel as good as I did last Saturday. Not a single person in the world could ever do that for me. Not like she did.

So, I don't do anything at all. Except helplessly give in to temptation whenever my desire stirs again.

By Friday, my cock is burning terribly, and also quite red. I only know because I looked in the mirror on the way into the shower; otherwise there's no way I could ever see that part of myself. I try my best to soothe the ache with a cold pack afterwards.

On Saturday morning, I find myself suspiciously eyeing my phone, just in case Eve calls to confirm our appointment. Time seems to slow down, the closer I get to the moment of truth. By eleven, the phone finally rings, and just like last week, I can hardly get a word out when I answer.

"Hello, Jamie?" Eve says.

I want to say hi, but all that comes out is a weird, forced grunt.

"How are you doing? Just wanted to confirm our session for four o'clock. We're all good, yeah?" she asks.

I close my eyes and try to breathe. My cock is so hard, it's getting chafed by my underwear. Jesus. How will I ever face her like this? I should tell her 'no'. I should make some excuse, maybe pretend like I've got some other plans. Then again, she knows I don't have plans like normal people do, because I never go anywhere and don't socialise. It was probably all in that bloody booking form she kept referring to during our first session!

"Okay. Four o'clock," I hear myself say instead.

"Lovely. I'm looking forward to seeing you again!" she chirps.

"Okay, bye!" I say, then bite my tongue. *I love you.*

The line goes silent again. Shit. Once again, I simply couldn't do the right thing. The poor girl has no idea what's really going on. If she did, she'd be wise never to set foot in my flat ever again.

* *Eve* *

It's been an interesting week. My schedule has been slowly filling up with more appointments. And thanks to my experiences with Jamie last Saturday, I'm starting to develop my own style now. I've figured out how to get people to open up. I don't try to hide my empathy, but lean into it. When things get emotional, I let it happen. It's been a relief, and most clients have found it very helpful, even cathartic.

In-person feedback from my clients has included the phrases: 'shoulder to cry on', 'great listener', 'someone who cares' many times over. As a result, I'm starting to feel like this job *will* work out after all.

I just have one big problem: if I don't convince Jamie to switch to someone else for his next session, I'll be shit out of luck with Joy, who has decided already that she hates my guts. Okay, two problems: I've also been having a tough time forgetting about how good it felt to cuddle with him in the first place.

For a day or two, I was fine. Every time my imagination started to wander, I told myself that I was just being hormonal. Or that I just really liked the tactile experience of cuddling with someone as fat as him. That my bodily reactions were normal, and I should just try to focus on other things.

But then, the dreams started.

The sexy, sweaty, filthy-ass dreams that left me wanting so much more. Once or twice, I even woke up mid-orgasm, with glimpses of Jamie and I, fucking feverishly, still playing out in the back of my mind. Those same images would follow me around throughout every day, cropping up when I least expected them.

Maybe that's what Joy meant, though I doubt it. The woman is blunt. In the many strained interactions we've had since that fateful lecture from Saturday night, she never once touched upon the idea that I might have found Jamie attractive, and that that could prevent me from doing my job properly. In fact, it's been quite the opposite.

When she went over my report with me, she blurted out a few comments which on closer inspection seemed severely fat phobic and dismissive of him as a person. That's ironic, considering she's not exactly skinny herself.

Worse still, we're supposed to be in a *caring* profession! We're meant to be open minded and compassionate. That shit actually is spelled out pretty clearly in the *rules* she likes to refer to, but seemingly has never read herself.

So, in hindsight, my week is a mixed bag. And the light at the end of the tunnel, strangely, is my standing appointment with Jamie, later today.

I call him up late morning to confirm, and hearing his voice does funny things to me.

I'm nervous again; almost scared. And I'm also giddy and excited. Like a schoolgirl hyping herself up to meet her crush.

How am I supposed to feel about that observation? It's highly inappropriate. And I'm sure it's the last thing on *his* mind. He's a client who booked me for a professional service. That's all.

So, as I make my way to his front door later in the

afternoon, I can feel myself getting unusually tense. Like, maybe I shouldn't be here? Maybe I'm taking advantage of the situation; putting him into a scenario that is bound to drag up sexual thoughts and feelings in me, whereas he's just trying to get help with his emotional problems.

Shit. Am I a sexual predator?

But it's too late for second-thoughts. I ring the doorbell and wait, all the while repeating one simple mantra in my head: don't get horny; don't get horny; don't get horny.

He opens the door and gives me room to enter. I force a smile.

"Hi!"

Don't get horny. Don't get horny!

I put my bag down on the coffee table and approach him with both arms outstretched for a hug. He leans down slightly and tentatively places his arm around my shoulder.

I can't stop myself from deeply inhaling his scent and closing my eyes while we embrace.

I'm home. Fuck knows what *that's* supposed to mean, but it's all I can think about.

"How have you been?" I ask.

He pulls away from me and shrugs. He's avoiding eye contact with me again. I guess it takes time to get back into a more comfortable dynamic.

"I've had a week."

Pfft, yeah. I've had a week too.

"There's something different…" I remark, while

looking around the room.

Indeed, his place looks tidier than last time. Even he does.

He doesn't give me any hint, though.

"Did you get a haircut?" I ask him.

He runs his hand through his trimmed hair and blushes. "Yeah."

"Looks good." I smile. "I like it!"

His cheeks darken further. It's adorable. I keep that particular observation to myself.

"So, why don't you tell me what else you've been up to since we last saw each other?" I suggest, while taking a seat in the same spot on the sofa. *My spot,* as I've started thinking of it already.

He lets out a muffled groan while he lowers himself onto the couch beside me. *His spot.*

"Well, I sent out your feedback form after you left. Took me a while to figure out what to write, though."

"Yeah, thanks so much for that!" I rest my hand on the empty sofa cushion between us, palm up. He glances at it and after a few seconds of hesitation, places his on top. I wrap my fingers around his and finally, I can breathe again. "I should mention, we don't get to see the actual comments. That goes straight to the supervisors."

"Want to know what I wrote?" he asks.

"Sure."

"I wrote that… I wrote that you're great at your work. That you changed my outlook on life within that first session."

Emotions bubble up and form a lump in my throat. "Aw, really?"

"Really."

"I'm so glad to be able to help. You're a wonderful guy. There's no reason you should be so hard on yourself all the time." There, I've blurted something out without thinking it through again. He never told me he's hard on himself, though it's blatantly obvious. That's something I picked up from the booking form, which he himself claims he barely remembers filling out...

I glance at Jamie from the corner of my eye and find his lower lip trembling a little. That prompts me to turn around all the way and fold my leg underneath me just to add a little height and get me closer to his level.

"What do you feel like doing today?" I whisper, while placing my hand on his shoulder.

"I don't know." His expression tenses and he shakes his head.

"We can start like last week. And then we'll see," I suggest.

He shrugs.

Just like last time, once I kneel beside him and invite him into my embrace, he capitulates. A weight lifts off my shoulders as we just breathe and experience the moment. Something tells me he feels the same way.

"Do you want to tell me what changed in your outlook this week?" I say.

He sighs. "It's rather stupid."

"I will never judge you. Trust me," I whisper, while caressing his back. I won't. Unlike Joy, who seems to judge everyone and most of all herself, probably.

He snuggles his face into the crook of my neck and sighs deeply again. It tickles beautifully and makes the hair on my arms stand up.

"While spending time with you, I realized that *everyone* has the same kind of doubts and insecurities, in some measure or other."

"So true." I tighten my grip on him and let bliss wash over me. I should probably say something profound and insightful right now, but I just can't get the words out. Inconveniently, the funny position I find myself in just to reach him properly is also doing a number on my back, causing me to shuffle from one leg to the other, desperate to find relief from the twinge in my spine.

"Are you okay?" he asks.

"My back's a little stiff. Nothing to worry about."

One of his hands slips down my back and rests halfway down, as if he knows exactly where the ache is. Then, he grips me firmly and hoists me up and onto his lap.

Don't get horny, dammit!

Fuck. This is all kinds of inappropriate, but it's also so perfect. Considering the size difference between us, it's actually the ideal way for us to cuddle without either of us having to strain too much.

I close my eyes and melt into him with my arms wrapped around his neck while he engulfs me in a great big bear hug. So good. So comforting.

"Better?" His voice cracks.

I can hardly get a word out. Better. And so much worse.

"Yeah," I whisper, while I rest my head on his shoulder.

The way he's cradling me in his arms, I simultaneously feel safe, cared for, and also mind-blowingly horny. I try not to focus on that latter part. I'm sure he isn't. God, this is so wrong.

Underneath me, I can feel his chest expand and contract with each of his breaths, kind of shallow and urgent. Anxiety, probably. This is new to both of us.

"I needed this after the week I've had," I mumble. This prompts him to hold me even tighter and nuzzle my hair. Now I can feel every exhale of his against my scalp too. My entire body is alight with sensations I have no use for. The best I can do is to practice what I preach normally, and just feel my feelings and wait for them to pass.

I loosen my grip on his neck and run my fingers through his hair. It's quite a bit shorter than last week. It suits him. And it feels really nice against my fingertips.

"Tell me about your week," he says. His voice is still raw. Although this really isn't the time or place, I remember what he said earlier. How I'd shown him that everyone has their own challenges. Who knows, it might be useful for him if I open up more? If nothing else, it'll build some rapport.

"Joy, my supervisor, is a stupid cow."

He chuckles briefly. "Aren't they all?"

"Considering the industry we're in, I would have

expected a little more compassion and self awareness."

"What happened?"

I shouldn't tell him everything. At least not until the end of the session. It'll only ruin things.

But does it really matter? If it's going to get ruined anyway, maybe I should just rip the band aid off.

I shift uneasily from one side to the other, while trying to find something appropriate to say. His thighs tense underneath me. His great big squishy thighs. Which I'm sitting on.

Do not get fucking horny!

It's hard not to. Impossible. His arms tighten some more while he also readjusts in his seat. His well-padded body ripples beneath me, amplifying every move of his. I slip just a little bit, my buttocks end up dangerously close to--

Jamie's breaths speed up further. As do mine. I can't think anymore and as such I can't react to what's going on.

Don't. Get. Oh God!

I barely realise what's happening. His arms, stronger than I ever imagined they would be, hold me captive. His hips tremble. His big belly shudders into my side. I want to touch it so badly. I want to *feel* him. All of him. Every bit of the man he is.

As he starts to wheeze with every breath, a low growl escapes his throat. He's panting now.

We're still not *doing* anything. Not purposely so. But it's happening anyway.

I pull away and look at him. His gorgeous face,

eyebrows crinkled together. Sweat collecting on his forehead. Full moist lips, gasping for air. For love and for acceptance.

I was right. I should have never come here. I should have--

God, I was also wrong. He *is* equally affected by me. This is the worst. The best. Joy was right, even if she was wrong about the reasons.

There's nothing in the handbook preparing me for this. For how I feel. For how I can see him suffer. Tears of exertion stream down his face. He isn't moving; not really. He's doing everything possible to stop the unstoppable.

I grab his face with both hands and do the only thing I can think to do. The only thing that could make this better. I press my lips onto his. His eyes open in shock. He tries to protest, but instead of stopping me, his hands end up on my back, slipping downward, onto my arse. He tugs at me, grinding me into him, crying and moaning into my mouth, while my tongue seeks to soothe his.

We kiss in a manner in which I've never been kissed before. Full of yearning and desperation and relief.

"Baby," I mumble into his lips. "Baby, I've got you. It's okay."

His climax is over before it even starts. A precious, forbidden moment, which we never should have shared at all. His shoulders slacken, and his thighs relax beneath me. So much tension, released within mere seconds.

I should stop. Apologise. Excuse myself and leave immediately. And then I should call him later and beg him not to write any of this stuff into the feedback for this session.

And yet, I continue to kiss him. And he continues to kiss me back. And time seems to stand still. Once his breaths calm, and his movements slow, I draw away from our mutual make-out session and look him in the eye again.

"I'm so fucking fired."

He presses his lips together and just stares at me. "I... You... I'm sorry!"

I put my hand on his cheek and run my thumb across his bottom lip like I've wanted to do since last week. "I'm going to get fired and I don't even care."

"I can't believe this is happening," he mumbles, while shaking his head.

"Oh, it happened."

"I mean... You... God, you're beautiful. All kinds of amazing."

"So are you." I'm not even lying. Looking at him now, I can clearly see it. He's a precious person, too good for this world.

But, the calm doesn't last because he soon tenses up again. His face contorts into a painful frown. His shoulders tighten and his hands ball into fists.

"What's wrong?" I whisper, running my fingers through his hair.

He shakes his head again, refusing to look me in the eye.

"You can tell me *anything*," I remind him.

His eyes wander around the room, while his breaths quicken again. "I'm so… So ashamed," This latest confession sounds more like an expression of physical pain. It probably is, to be honest.

"I'm the one who should be ashamed," I respond.

He scoffs. "Yeah, you probably should."

My cheeks burn up, but I don't let his words derail me. It's confession time. For both of us.

"I feel like I willed this to happen," I say.

His eyes are on me like darts. "What?!"

I take a deep breath and focus solely on maintaining eye contact with him. As I exhale slowly, I find the words to explain. "I have been dreaming of having sex with you since I left your place last week. Obviously, it seems like you picked up on my energy, and one thing led to another…"

"What? No! *I* have been fantasising about *you* all week. You should have stopped me. You should have--" He's fighting back tears so furiously, I wonder what he thinks will happen if he lets them out.

"So, we've both been lusting after each other," I conclude. "That's not so bad then."

"Not so bad?" His hands find my upper arms and grip them firmly, as if he's trying to shake some sense into me. "What the fuck is wrong with you?"

He's obviously upset and lashing out, so I'm not going to take that personally. Instead, I keep looking at him with my eyebrows raised, waiting for the silence to become so loaded he tells me what's really going on underneath all this bluster.

"Last week I couldn't figure out why you would even come here. And once you arrived and saw... why you would ever stay. Why you would carry on and *touch* me, as if..."

He inhales deeply, and the tears start to flow freely.

"Why would you--"

My gaze softens as I watch him cry. And soon, my eyes are moist too. I simply can't help it. This is how it has always worked for me. I tend to absorb and mirror what I see. Unfortunately that tends to make people feel bad, because they think they're hurting me somehow. They're not. It's just a reflex.

"I'm so sorry!" he sobs.

"Why *wouldn't* I come? You called me. And why would I leave, when it was so obvious that you needed me to be here?" I whisper.

"Why aren't you leaving now? When I've... I've..."

"Jamie, we're in the same boat. How could I leave you?" I ask.

"Because I don't deserve your company!" he complains, while glaring at me through his tears.

I gently run the back of my fingers across his wet cheek. He flinches and squeezes his eyes shut, but he doesn't protest. I think deep down he's afraid that I'll take the bait and stop what I'm doing.

"Why not?" I know I'm pushing and prodding him right in the gooey bits. I *know* it. But it's necessary. I must know what's inside; and he must let it out.

"Because I'm despicable! A disgusting pervert.

Taking advantage of the situation. Of you here," he rants.

"Are you, though?"

He opens his eyes again and stares at me.

"I'm a grown woman. I make my own choices. I could have said something to deescalate the situation. I could have left if I wanted to."

"Jesus Christ, Eve!"

"But instead, I decided to kiss you. And I'd do it again in a heartbeat."

His lips part again. I can't look away. I can't do a damn thing, actually. I can't get up, and not because he won't let me, but because I'm completely unwilling to change a single thing about this situation right here. Me. Sitting in his lap. With my arse crushing down on his spent erection.

Well okay, perhaps I would change *one* thing about our situation. I would like an orgasm of my own. It feels too early to ask for that, though.

His right hand loosens its grip on my arm and starts travelling upwards, ever so slowly. Upwards over my shoulder, and onto the side of my neck. Fingers curl around back, threading through my hair.

"Jamie. You turn me on so much," I whisper, just about loud enough for him to hear.

His fingertips dig into the back of my neck as his hand twitches. His eyes are locked onto mine.

"Impossible. This can't be happening," he mumbles to himself.

He looks like he's seen a ghost. Or an angel. The fear

and anger I saw in him only moments earlier are fading fast, and being replaced by wonder.

"I shouldn't have come here for a session today. I should have cancelled, and then turned up with a bottle of wine and a pack of condoms," I say. "I should have laid it all out there."

"You can't just say stuff like that. It's not fair," he says.

"I mean it." I carefully place my arms around his neck again, my heart racing out of control now.

"You cannot like me like that." He brushes an errant lock of hair out of my face.

"I do, though." I smile.

He's too stunned to reciprocate.

"You can't! Nobody has *ever* liked me like that. I'm not fit for purpose; I..." he stammers.

"You're so very special. I knew it straightaway last week."

He grimaces again. "I've spent the entire week beating off to the memory of being allowed to touch you."

That makes me grin even more. "You think I didn't?"

"You wouldn't!"

"I did." I briefly bite my bottom lip while glancing down at his mouth. I know what his lips taste like now. But maybe I should kiss him again just to make sure.

"But... I'm hideous!" he complains.

"What, you think only skinny people deserve to have sex?" I ask. "You're fucking gorgeous, Jamie!

Everything about you is…" I inhale sharply through my teeth while looking down at his chest, his big belly, straining against his t-shirt with every hurried breath.

"You're lying." His accusation only makes me double down.

"I want to fuck you, Jamie. I want for you to fill me up, bareback, and show me everything I've been yearning for all week!" I hiss.

His eyes flag momentarily. That was unfair of me, I know. But maybe it was exactly what he needed to hear to get out of his own way. Sometimes the best way to get past a painful problem is to just rip the band aid off.

Plus, I'm so damn wet right now, I'll lose my mind if I don't get some relief soon.

"I don't want to dance around the issue anymore, you hear me?" I demand.

"Okay…"

"I *want* you. Right now. And if you want me too, you just have to say so."

The few seconds of silence between us is so tense, I can almost feel the air crackle with electricity.

"I want you, Eve." His voice cracks.

This final admission tickles something deep inside my chest. Like a lightning strike, it changes everything it hits forever. I smile and get up off of him, gesturing at him to follow. "Bedroom. Now!"

It occurs to me that I've never left the living room so I don't even know the way. So I wait while he struggles to get up off the sofa. In the meantime, I remember to pick up my phone and clock out of our session, hopefully preventing both of us from getting into any more trouble.

Finally, he's on his feet and completely out of breath again. His fingers tremble when I take his hand.

"Lead the way, handsome," I say.

He does. Slowly. Stumbling along the way through the almost too-narrow hallway and into the bedroom at the end. I'm not sure what's waiting for me in there, but luckily it doesn't disappoint.

His bed is massive, just like him. I get on top first and kneel down while making a start on my clothes.

He pauses at the sidelines.

"Clothes off, baby," I tell him.

"I can't," he whispers.

Okay, maybe that's a step too far as yet. I smile at him and beckon him over, then I slip my shirt over my head and unhook my bra.

He sits on the bed, turns to watch, and freezes.

"Jamie, do you want to touch me?" I ask sweetly.

* Jamie *

"Do you want to touch me?" she asks.

Jesus-fucking-Christ. I don't know where to look. At her tits; perky and yet full to perfection? Or at her hips, which are slowly coming into view while she slowly but surely peels off her jeans?

Or maybe her reddened lips, which have been begging for me to kiss them ever since she broke away on the sofa earlier.

I don't even know how this happened. How did we go from a professional cuddle session to me rubbing myself raw against her backside until I jizzed myself? And her, rather than fighting me off and running for her life, kissing me. Kissing me so deeply, I'm not sure I'll ever catch my breath after that.

The thing she doesn't seem to realise is that I'm *really* not fit for purpose. I've been jerking off a lot this past week. It's all I've done. That, and drinking too much beer to try and dull my inappropriate desire for her.

I'm a nervous wreck. Over-caffeinated, slightly buzzed, because I already finished a six-pack of beer before she showed up, and aching pretty much all over, especially on my dick which I've rubbed sore. It's no wonder I keep crying like a fucking pussy in front of her. My nerves are shot. I'm broken; defective; and so very ashamed of myself right now. Because no matter what she says, she doesn't deserve *this*. She deserves a Prince Charming. A fairytale romance. An Adonis, who will pleasure her in ways I couldn't even dream of.

Yet she's asking for *me*? I don't even know what to do! That there on the sofa was my first ever kiss. In my mid-fucking-thirties, and that was my first kiss. I'm a fat fucking pathetic virgin; that's what I am. Doesn't she realize that?

"Baby, come lie with me," she says.

I try to breathe, and close my eyes just for a moment to ward off a dizzy spell.

I can't refuse, can I? I mean, I want to do everything

she asks. I want to make her *happy*. But I know that I can't possibly achieve such a lofty goal.

The mattress dips down behind me and I feel her hands on me again. Running up my back, over my shoulders, and down my chest… My heart is pounding and my head is throbbing. She melts into me from behind and plants a few soft kisses on the side of my neck.

"If you want me to stop, I will," she says. "Talk to me."

"I'm so scared of disappointing you. I mean, I *know* I'll disappoint you. It's like I'm staring at certain death." Jamie from one-and-a-half cuddle sessions ago would have never admitted to this. But, something tells me it's exactly the sort of thing she wants to hear.

"What if you're staring at enlightenment; you just don't know it yet?" she asks.

She wraps one of her arms tightly across the top of my chest, rests her head on my shoulder and lets the other hand travel further down, pausing once she reaches my man boob. It's such an ugly part of me. Overgrown, saggy, more unworthy of her touch than everything else she's explored so far.

As a result, I freeze, and my throat closes up further. But rather than shy away from it, she grows more confident and persistent in her explorations. She squeezes it, finds the nipple and rolls it gently between her thumb and index finger, while whispering filthy things in my ear.

"You're so fucking sexy, Jamie. Look at this! Feel

this big juicy tit of yours. I bet it tastes good, doesn't it? Will you let me taste it?"

I was already hard. So very sore, but so very hard all the same. Now I'm just about ready to explode again. The entire situation is just so embarrassing though, I can't quite force myself into action yet.

Undeterred, she carries on caressing and fondling me, until she reaches the other man boob. This time, when she squeezes my nipple--just a little harder than the last time--I squirm in my seat, desperate for more.

"So good," I groan.

"Yeah, it is! So hot. Can you feel how hard my nipples are? Grazing against your back when I move. I bet you can feel it through your shirt."

I frown and try to breathe. Yeah. Yeah, I can feel them! Like little darts, they are.

"Do you want to touch them? Maybe even kiss them for me?" she asks.

I reach for her hand with mine, guiding her back to my left nipple.

"Harder," I growl.

She does what I ask, and simultaneously rubs up against my back. Oh, this is the best feeling! If only my cock wasn't hurting so badly, chafing against my damp underwear. I should do something about that... *Or, maybe...*

No, you filthy bastard! You can't ask her to--

Eve nibbles on my earlobe, sending shivers down the side of my neck.

It doesn't matter what she does, somehow the

sensations end up straight in my balls. They're tight already, preparing to shoot another load. After the near-constant abuse I've put them through all week, I'm surprised they're still functional.

"Lie down next to me," she whispers. "I want to see your face while I play with you!"

Why she would want that is beyond me. My great big pancake face isn't anything worth looking at. But I can't fight her demands anymore. She has me wrapped around her little finger. Plus, I'd be able to look at *her*. And that's a prospect I cannot resist.

I push back further onto the bed while Eve moves out of the way and kneels beside me. I let myself fall onto my back, waiting breathlessly for her to get comfortable in the crook of my arm.

A naked angel in my bed. In my arms. I must be dreaming.

But, I'm not. Because in my dream, she wouldn't be touching me like she's doing right now. Even my fantasies aren't *that* depraved. But there she is, with her hand slipping in underneath my t-shirt and grazing the bare skin of my lower belly. It tickles a little, but mostly, it just terrifies me. Because with that little action she will have figured out just how unworthy I really am.

"I love this," she whispers. "I adore the softness of your skin."

Even though all my blood has been pooling in my crotch all week, I seem to still have enough leftover to blush deeply. Just when I want to argue, she takes my breath away again by rubbing her hand up my entire torso and finding my nipple again. This time skin-on-skin.

Oh God. I never knew how good this could feel.

It doesn't seem to matter that my shoulders and neck hurt quite a bit while I'm on my back like this. Or that I'm getting more and more short of breath. None of it matters. Because I could very happily suffocate on my own tongue right now and still die with a smile on my face.

"Eve," I wheeze.

"Yes, baby."

God, I love it when she calls me baby. I love *her*.

"Show me how to please you," I ask.

I'm sure to disappoint her no matter what I try, but maybe with the right kind of instructions…

"Touch me," she says, while getting up, wiggling her body against me and placing her thigh across one of mine.

It occurs to me that so far I've just been lying there like a corpse with my arms limp on the mattress. Embarrassing. I tighten one arm around her, pulling her into my side and caressing her naked skin. Any part of her within reach. Her arm; her back; her side; the side of her hip…

She grinds into my leg and moans deliciously. I wish I knew what to do. How to make *her* feel good. I do have one idea, but I'm still too scared to suggest it.

Meanwhile she doesn't seem to have any of the same worries or fears. She just *does* stuff. Tweaking my nipples, one after the other, until I'm covered in goose bumps. Running her fingernails across my chest. Kissing whatever part of me she can get to; in this instance, my chest, through my t-shirt. Would be nice to know what *that* feels like without clothes on…

A part of me wants to just lie here and enjoy it, but that seems selfish. So, I feel the tension in my chest grow and grow, until finally I no longer have a choice but to blurt out my dumbass idea.

"Can I eat you out?" I ask.

She whimpers my name while grinding her crotch into my leg, almost as if she can't help it. She seems to be enjoying herself already, so I almost backtrack, when she leans up on her elbow and smiles down at me.

"Oh, would you?"

"I would do anything for you," I say. Shocked at the candidness of my own admission, as well as how I absolutely and totally mean it. She's surprised too, judging by how wide her eyes become just for a moment, before that earlier naughty smile makes a comeback.

"Sit on me, goddess!" I say.

A moan escapes her lips. Her sweet, bright red, slightly trembling lips. I've never seen a more beautiful sight than this gorgeous woman, so aroused, she couldn't keep it to herself if she wanted to.

As such, I'm stunned into silence as she gets up and carefully straddles my face, lowering her hips until her wet, shaven pussy makes contact with my lips. I instinctively grab her hips, marvelling at the smoothness of her skin.

Oh my God. The smell of her sex is intoxicating. I kiss her, softly at first. Then I try to feel my way around her vulva with my lips. I don't remember much of high school anatomy class, so I have to go on instinct. And I let her guide me.

There are so many folds; some big; some small. All of them covered in skin so soft, it could make me weep.

Fuck it. They *are* making me weep.

But this time they're tears of pure joy. She tastes sweet and salty and irresistible all at once. Her hips start to rock above me, guiding my tongue into the deepest crease, until I find a secret hiding inside. A hard nub more towards the front of her cleft, which makes her twitch and squeal when I flick my tongue across it.

Could it be that I've just found her clitoris?

I do it again. And again. Enjoying how her thighs tremble beside my face, and her breaths grow quicker. Every so often, a little squeal escapes her lips, setting my soul alight.

With a subtle twitch of her pelvis, she soon urges me to go in deeper. My tongue finds the source of all this tasty nectar I've been lapping up. Her vagina is slick with the juices of her arousal.

It's so soft and slippery. I wonder what it would be like to enter her properly. As soon as the thought crosses my mind, one of my hands lets go of her thigh and finds its way downward on my own body, lightly touching my rock hard erection. It feels so wrong to steal this little reward, and yet I can't help myself.

Even though I'm feeling myself through my clothes,

it still stings a little. But it's a delicious sort of pain. And gives me the confidence--or desperation--to grab her ass with my other hand, while really going at her pussy with my mouth.

At first I was just licking it, now I'm fucking her with my tongue.

She seems to love it; telling me so with every moan and whimper.

It occurs to me that I've had my eyes squeezed shut this whole time. When I finally open them and look up at her, I find that she's already gazing down at me. Past her ripe breasts and toned stomach, she's staring at me with an expression on her face which I'm not sure how to interpret.

Hunger. Greed?

Yes, that's it.

She lowers herself onto my face the rest of the way, until my entire tongue is inside of her all the way. Then she grinds back and forth a few times. Just enough to create some friction inside.

"So good," she moans. "You're killing me!"

I'm beyond caring about how any of this looks now. After fumbling with my waistband, I finally slip my hand into my underwear and grab myself more firmly. It still hurts, obviously. But that's not going to stop me from cumming again.

Eve's movements on top of my face speed up. She's really face fucking me now. My jaw is getting stiff, but none of it matters.

A tongue is much smaller than a dick though, isn't it?

Will this be enough to satisfy her?

I try to match her rhythm, and carry on working on myself. She's given me too much already; the least I can do is finish without asking any more of her. But just when I get used to what we're doing, she switches it up and guides my mouth back to the front. To her clitoris. By now, her formerly strong thighs are trembling a little.

"Suck on it, veeery gently!" she instructs.

When I do, she shudders into me and almost loses her balance. I let go of myself and firmly grab her arse, steadying her above me. We share a moment of eye contact. Funny, how one look can express so much.

One of her hands rests on her thigh, with the other, she starts caressing my damp hair. It's beautiful. Everything about her is, anyway. But this little gesture. It's so loving. So heart wrenching. I almost choke on my own breath and carry on staring into her beautiful green eyes.

But I don't give up like I normally would have. I do exactly as she asked; sucking so very softly on that hard little lump in between her folds until she can't stay quiet any longer.

She's moaning with every breath now. With every move I make. Her left hand finds mine at the back of her hips, and squeezes down hard on it. The other is still playing with my hair, but growing more and more uncoordinated.

I have no doubt that she's getting close. And it's too good to be true.

My earlier thoughts about finishing myself off

quickly have long since been wiped away. My sole focus is on her. Her pleasure. Her happiness. Her impending orgasm which will lead to my redemption.

Maybe she was right. I was staring enlightenment in the face without knowing it. And now that it's within reach, I can hardly remember or understand why I fought so hard against this moment. I almost let fear win; and for what? I would have lost out on this moment. The single best moment of my entire life so far.

She's grinding into my chin again. Her folds surround my mouth; the entire lower half of my face. It's hard to breathe, but I don't care. I wish I could do this forever.

As long as she's pleased, all feels right in this world.

I suckle on her clit again. Softly, persistently. She trembles and cries and digs her fingernails into my hand. I almost stop. *Almost.*

But a little voice in my head tells me not to. It tells me to carry on and see this through to the end. She freezes above me. A fresh wave of wetness ends up in my mouth; even sweeter than the last.

She falls apart; moaning loudly, with her eyes tightly shut and her right hand on her tit, squeezing down on it as she grinds into my face one last time. And then…

Then there's silence. Save for the gasps for air and relentless drum beat of my heart in my own ears.

She opens her eyes and looks down on me as a changed person. Yeah, this is what enlightenment feels like.

Despite the near-constant pain in my crotch. Despite the ache in my chest, which has worsened ever since I lay down on my back. None of it matters, because I made her cum. *Me.*

Her eyes are full of wonder, mixed in with something else; something alien, as she continues to gaze down at me. I feel so seen, but in a good way.

"Jamie, that was…"

She doesn't have to finish her sentence, because I already agree.

That was amazing.

She straightens her back a little and starts to get off me. I almost don't want to let go of her thighs, but I'm getting lightheaded, so I let it happen.

Rather than get dressed and leave, she lowers herself next to me again. Once again, I'm in a place I never thought I would be. In my shitty apartment, in my bed, with a goddess in my arms. She wraps her arms around me as tightly as they'll go. Giving it all I've got, I turn around to face her. It's weird, and my body doesn't really cooperate. But I'm so spent now--almost as if I was the one having the orgasm instead of her--that I don't really care how bad this looks.

She doesn't care either, from the looks of her.

Eve starts to peel my t-shirt off my belly. Slowly, but surely, more and more of me comes into view. Not that I can see, because it's too far down, but I can feel the cool air against my skin. It makes me feel more vulnerable than I already was.

"Don't be shy," she whispers.

I find myself captivated by her sparkly green eyes. What an absolutely gorgeous woman she is.

And what a complete beast I am.

"I don't get why you want this," I mumble.

She just smiles, and my heart skips a bunch of beats.

"We have a chemistry together which I've never encountered before," she says.

I try to analyse her words. She's obviously not a virgin like me. A woman as beautiful as her would have had plenty of lovers to compare me to. Plenty of better options. And yet...

The intensity of my own feelings towards her is easily explained away. Desperation. Experiencing female affection for the very first time.

But what could possibly be her justification?

"In case it wasn't apparent from that bloody intake form..." I start, take a deep breath, and then just stare at her with my heart in my throat, instead of finishing my thought.

She rests her hand on my cheek, giving me the courage to carry on.

"I've never, *you know*..." I say.

"Today's the day," she says.

I don't have the words to respond to that. I pleasured her with my mouth. Surely, she's done now? Yet her eyes are still full of greed.

"Take your clothes off, baby," she whispers.

I really don't want to, and yet... The intense look in her eyes continues to tempt me out of my comfort zone.

"Take your clothes off and fuck me," she urges. "I already told you I wanted it. Bareback."

An errant groan escapes my lips. Even my wildest dreams are never as sexy as that very blunt, very clear invitation. Good God, how do I resist?

Why would I even want to?

I thought I'd already achieved enlightenment when she orgasmed against my mouth, yet her eyes continue to promise me *more*.

And so, fighting my body and mind every step of the way, I slowly roll onto my side away from her and try to get up. First on all fours, then onto my knees. The t-shirt she'd partially pulled off me falls back down, forcing me to start on it again.

Eve, still on her back, with one hand folded underneath her head and the other idly stroking her naked body, watches with a look of horny anticipation on her face. Eyes wide and greedy. Lips, still bright red and slightly parted. Her chest rises and falls in quick succession as her breaths speed at the sight of me. At some point the hair band must have fallen out of her hair, so it's now spread around the bed underneath her, and sticking to the damp skin of her neck and shoulders.

My goddess, she's pleased. Still high after her orgasm, and yet not fully satisfied.

If this is what she wants, then who am I to refuse?

I pull my top off quickly, before I get the chance to chicken out. She licks her lips and reaches for me, squeezing and fondling my bare belly. If it wasn't so bizarre, I'd say she's enjoying it. Enjoying my body.

I've never been touched like this. Never. Until barely an hour ago, I'd never been kissed either, I remind myself.

Today's the day. That's what she said.

And so, I pull down my trousers too. It's a bit of a struggle to get out of them, and my cum stained underwear, but I manage it somehow. Once I'm fully exposed, I feel disconnected. From myself; from the entire situation; from her. Like I'm not really here, and this isn't really my body. I suppose it's better than the alternative; pure terror and utter humiliation.

She gestures at me to join her; to get on top of her. Only when I start to lower myself onto her, and her arms wrap around my neck do I seem to relax. I close my eyes and breathe. God, I'm so hard. So hard and so sore. And it feels so good to be here with her. In her arms, I'm safe. Just like last week during our first session. But also not at all the same.

And Eve; she starts to kiss me. Her sweet lips seek me out hungrily. As if she doesn't notice or care that I'm covered in pussy juices. She slips her tongue into my mouth without hesitation or delay. Short, urgent breaths are the only thing interrupting our feverish kisses.

Underneath me, her athletic body seems to come alive all over again. She wiggles and writhes up into me.

She pauses briefly, turns her head and kisses my neck now. "God, Jamie, your body is perfection."

Her words confuse, because clearly she couldn't have

said that. But her hands don't leave any room for doubt as they explore my sides, rubbing, grabbing, squeezing and caressing me all at once.

She's all hands and I love it.

I'm hers to play with and she knows it.

And I can feel the inevitable creep up on me again.

No matter how many times I've cum this week. No matter how tired I am. How nervous I should be about all of this. All I can do is follow her lead.

She tries to spread her legs for me, but it's difficult with me in the way. I raise myself onto my knees and finally we manage it together. My big belly is in the way, or at least I think it is. But she does something, wiggling down and tilting her hips up at me, and before I know it she's managed to grab my cock, almost sending the remainder of my self control into a tailspin.

Relief is so close I can taste it.

My body starts to move with a mind of its own as well, pushing, grinding, seeking her out on pure instinct. She guides me in and before I know it I'm surrounded by her tight hot pussy and I lose it.

Tears stream down my face. This much anticipated and desired moment has arrived without warning or much build-up. I don't have time to reconsider. Or do much thinking at all. I can only act.

She moans my name and scratches her fingernails across my shoulders when I push into her as deeply as I can.

My body isn't used to moving like this, but it's still happening. With as much of my weight on my arms and knees as I can manage, I try to settle into a sensible rhythm.

But there's nothing sensible about the situation unfolding in my bed today.

We're animals, acting purely on instinct.

Those groans filling the air; the gasps for air; it's freaky. Primal. Something that sounds less like a porn clip and more like something you'd find on Animal Planet.

It's amazing and beautiful.

Like her moans. Her voice sets my soul alight and makes me speed up and slow down all at once.

I'm not detached anymore. This body, it's my own again. Bigger than I would want it to be, but not if she likes it this way.

And she seems to love it. She seems to not be able to get enough of me. The way she keeps touching me.

Her left hand finds my nipple again, manipulating it like she did earlier. And that's almost too much.

"Eve, fucking hell!" I growl.

"Jamie, don't stop!" she demands.

I don't. I couldn't possibly stop this freight train now that it's finally in motion.

I keep grinding into her, destroying her beautiful little body underneath me.

The harder I go at it, the less I'm able to keep my weight off her, and interestingly, the more out of control she gets. The louder her moans, until they're almost muffled screams. The firmer her touch on my love handles and chest. The harder she bites down on my neck.

"Oh fuck, Jamie! You're the best," she cries.

I know that couldn't possibly be true, but it snaps something in me anyway. Like a switch that's been flipped. All the soreness and nerves and doubts fade. Everything we've been building up to comes to a head. Every bit of pain and pleasure collects somewhere in my pelvis, growing and buzzing out of control until there's nowhere else for it to go but out.

My balls tighten and my cock convulses inside her slick pussy, dumping a big load of cum into her tight little pussy.

And that's still not the end of it. Normally when I jerk off, I always stop right at the point of no return. I freeze. It's not that I don't want to go on, it's just that normally my body doesn't let me.

Not so right now. Right now, with her arms tugging at me, her hips grinding up into me, I force myself through the inertia of my orgasm and carry on slamming into her. Once. Twice. Three times.

And a most unexpected thing happens. As I grow lightheaded, blinded by pleasure I've never known before, her movements change underneath me as well. I force my eyes open to look at her gorgeous face and find that she's smiling and crying and gasping for air all at once and it's the most amazing sight. It's transcendent. Life-changing.

Her pussy tightens around me, twitching, pulsating. And the expression on her face leaves no room for doubt. I've done it. I've made her cum again. I didn't even know that was possible, except maybe in porn. And even then, I figured they're faking.

So enamoured am I, that I forget all about how utterly shattered I am after my own orgasm, that I shift my weight onto one arm and start caressing her sweet flushed cheeks with my other hand while whispering sweet encouragements at her to comfort her.

"Jamie," she mouths.

God, I love it when she says my name. When she looks at me like this. When she touches me so full of warmth and understanding. When she makes me feel like I'm not alone.

"Jamie, please tell me we get to do this again. And again. Every day. Every night…"

I freeze and stop everything I'm doing. I think I even forget to breathe as I stare at her, trying to decipher the words that just escaped her red shapely lips.

"Of course," I stammer.

She wants to do it again? Every day; every night?

Her arms tighten around my neck and my heart barely knows what to do with that. With the entire situation, for that matter.

"Seeing as I'm fired anyway, there will be no more sessions. No bookings. No feedback. No bullshit. I'll have fuck-all to do all day, so maybe you wouldn't mind having me around more…" she says.

This sounds an awful lot like…

She smiles up at me. "You look confused."

It occurs to me that I had assumed that this experience; this forbidden moment we stole today would change her. That she wouldn't be the same chatty, cheerful person I've been thoroughly engrossed by ever since we first met last week. Nothing could be further from the truth.

She's still the same kind, sensitive, irresistible soul who first got me out of my shell.

"I guess I wasn't expecting this," I explain.

"Neither was I, but here we are."

* Eve *

I'm still weighed down by Jamie's big, luxurious body, when I just can't stay quiet anymore. I have to figure out if this experience today has affected him as deeply as it has me.

"I guess I wasn't expecting this," he tells me after I ask him if he wants to spend more time together.

It's not a confirmation, but it's not a refusal either. And he's not moving. So there's that.

The longer I spend looking into his eyes, the more comforted I feel. I'm not on the wrong track here, am I? He's open; completely unguarded.

I see affection in his gaze, maybe even love.

More than anything else, it's that same love I want from him. Again and again. I could feel it in every movement; in every touch throughout our experience just now.

I could feel what he felt. How intensely he reacted to me from the moment I first touched him last week.

Of course I was still trying to be professional back

then. And that ship has long since sailed. But in a way, nothing has really *changed*, either. I'm still equally enamoured by him. And he's still as raw and open and willing to give himself over to the process. To me.

That's what I want. More than anything else.

I want him in my life a lot more often than once a week. Not as a client. Not as a subject to be fixed and manipulated and cured. But as a man. To be loved and enjoyed and yes--fucked. I want to fuck his brains out.

I want to show him how he makes me feel every moment we spend together. I want to keep showing him until he can't help but feel what I feel too. Until we have a connection that goes both ways.

It should be possible, even if I've never encountered it before. But with him… I feel like we're already almost there.

"I…" he stares at me and loses his words again.

I can't blame him. It's hard for me to put my feelings into something coherent, and I normally wear my heart on my sleeve. And so I wait, patiently, while running my fingers through his hair and watching every little micro expression of his like a hawk.

I'm not a bad judge of character, am I? Everything I see, it's not just in my head. It's right bloody there in front of me. I can see that he loves it. I can see how he's changed in one short week, even if it's been hard for him to reconcile himself with it.

Imagine what we could achieve in a month?

"Eve, this makes no sense. I don't even understand it myself. And I won't blame you if you shut me down…"

he whispers.

"But?"

"But, I think… I think I'm hopelessly trapped. I wouldn't know how *not* to spend every waking moment thinking about you."

That makes me grin widely. I *knew* it.

"Same."

"Because, I think…" He takes a deep breath and looks at me with a thoughtful frown on his face. His deep brown eyes are so warm, they could make me weep all over again.

I think so too. Whatever you're going to say, I feel it too!

"I think I might love you." That statement comes out more like a question, but it doesn't matter. I can only imagine how hard it was for him to tell me that.

And as a result, I'm overflowing. With warmth. With excitement. With passion. I don't even know anymore. But it's all good.

I'm smiling. Tears are pooling in the corner of my eyes again, but they no longer bother me.

I grab his face and pull him down until his lips meet mine again. He still tastes salty after eating me out, and that makes it all the more special.

Fuck the repercussions. Screw everything. Objectively, I might have fucked up majorly today. I let my heart rule my head, and threw caution in the wind. But it was absolutely the right call to make. Because what I wanted more than anything in my life--more than a damn job--was this kind of connection and kinship. I needed to feel needed like I do right now.

"I love you too," I whisper at him.

Never before have I said these words to someone I know so little about, objectively. Never before have I meant them like I do right now. I already feel like I know everything I need to know about him; about us. And the rest, we'll figure out soon enough.

Somewhere in the distance, my phone rings. That'll be Joy, waiting to give me an earful.

I don't care anymore. It doesn't matter. This, right here, matters more than anything else in my life.

"Do you need to take that?" Jamie asks.

I shake my head. "I need you to kiss me again."

He smiles. A rare, most precious smile. It occurs to me that I've hardly seen him smile in all the time we've spent together so far. Something tells me that's about to change. Now that we've found each other, I'll try to give him reason to, any time we are together. To smile. To laugh. To kiss, caress, cuddle and so much more. Maybe I am too sensitive, most of the time. But I feel like with Jamie, that won't be a problem. Maybe he's too sensitive too, so we're exactly on the same page.

I wrap my arms around his neck and sigh deeply. His manly slightly sweet and spicy scent fills my nostrils and makes me lightheaded. This is what I want. What I need.

Every day and every night. For as long as he'll have me.

ABOUT THE AUTHOR

Dear Reader,

If you came across me in real life, you'd never guess the kind of filth I like to read and write. Cleverly disguised as a boring office worker, the drudgery of my 9-to-5 only because bearable because of my vivid and explicit imagination. I like fat guys and I cannot lie. In my world, bigger (fatter) is always better. It's been that way for as long as I can remember.

Thanks for reading this story, one of hopefully many of my published sexual fantasies. My stories revolve around one common theme: really big men and the women who can't help but lust for them.

Although I like porn just fine, it's nearly impossible to find it in the flavour that I desire. The written word allows me to explore a world of lush excess that mainstream adult entertainment just cannot provide. When I started writing, I soon discovered the beauty of having a catalog of erotica out there to satisfy my own lustful needs. This is a passion project more than a money-grab.

So, first and foremost, my writing is for me. But perhaps there are other women (or even men) out there who share my tastes; my fetishes and fantasies? My fascination with the larger male form, and sexualisation of food (especially overeating). If that sounds like something you'll wank off to, you've come to the right place.

xxx Hedonist

To find out more, check:

- ❖ eXplicitTales.com